The Moose is Loose!

by Mike Thaler • Pictures by Toni Goffe

SCHOLASTIC BOOK SERVICES

NEW YORK • TORONTO • LONDON • AUCKLAND • SYDNEY • TOKYO

ISBN 0-590-31291-X

Text copyright © 1980 by Michael C. Thaler. Illustrations copyright © 1980 by Toni Goffe. All rights reserved. Published by Scholastic Book Services, a Division of Scholastic Magazines, Inc.

12 11 10 9 8 7 6 5 4 3 2 1   11   0 1 2 3 4 5/8

One day the moose escaped from the zoo.

The Zoo Director called the world-famous detective,
Inspector Hippo Spotamoose.

Spotamoose agreed to take the case.

But he's going to have a hard time of it.

The moose is a master of disguise.

The Inspector cannot find the moose. Can you?

Day and night the Inspector looks for clues.

But no moose in sight.

No moose at the opera...

No moose at the ball game...

No moose at the Roller Disco...

The Inspector is puzzled.

But will he give up? NO!

Weeks pass. Still no luck.

Now it is winter. The weather is cold.

The moose's whereabouts are still unknown.

The Inspector cannot crack the case.

He goes back to the Zoo Director.

The great Inspector Spotamoose has
done it again! Merry Christmas!